TRAIN YOUR BRAIN

THINK LIKE AN ENGINEER

written by Alex Woolf

illustrated by David Broadbent

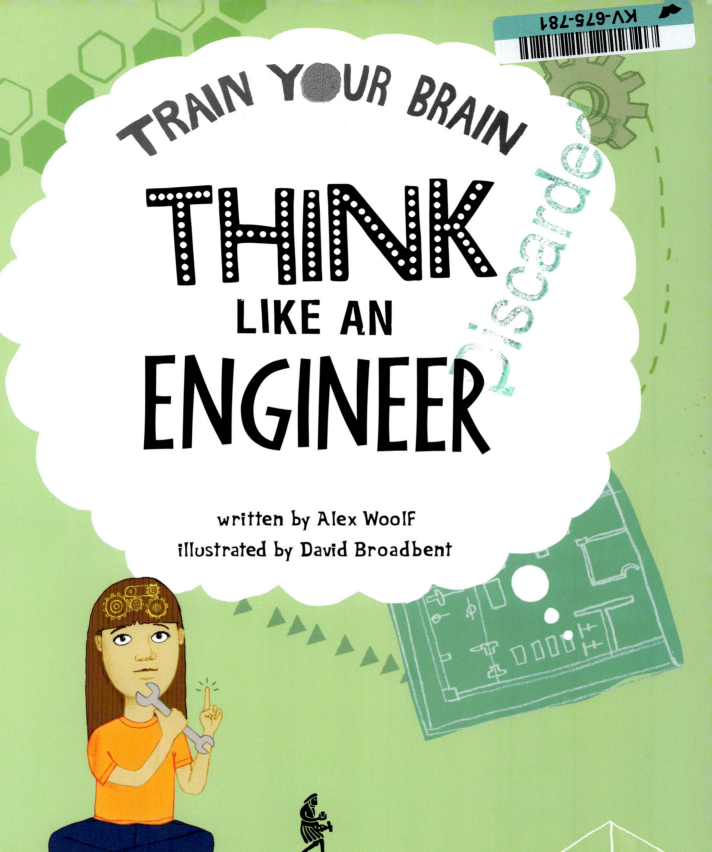

WAYLAND

First published in Great Britain in 2021 by Wayland
Copyright © Hodder and Stoughton, 2021

 Produced for Wayland by
White-Thomson Publishing Ltd
www.wtpub.co.uk

ISBN (HB): 978 1 5263 1652 3
ISBN (PB): 978 1 5263 1653 0
10 9 8 7 6 5 4 3 2 1

Series Designer: David Broadbent
All Illustrations by: David Broadbent

Printed in China

Wayland
An imprint of
Hachette Children's Group
Part of Hodder & Stoughton
Carmelite House
50 Victoria Embankment
London EC4Y 0DZ

An Hachette UK Company
www.hachettechildrens.co.uk

WEST NORTHAMPTONSHIRE COUNCIL	
60000498697	
Askews & Holts	
NC	

The activities described in this book should always be done in the presence of a trusted adult.
A trusted adult is a person (over 18 years old) in a child's life who makes them feel safe, comfortable and supported. It might be a parent, teacher, family friend, care worker or another adult.

Facts, figures and dates were correct when going to press.

A note from the author and publisher
In preparation of this book, all due care has been exercised with regard to the instructions, activities and techniques depicted. The publishers and author regret that they can accept no liability for any loss or injury sustained. Always get adult supervision and follow manufacturers' advice when using electric and battery-powered appliances.

Every effort has been made by the Publishers to ensure websites are suitable for children, that they are of the highest educational value, and that they contain no inappropriate or offensive material. However, because of the nature of the Internet, it is impossible to guarantee that the contents of these sites will not be altered. We strongly advise that Internet access is supervised by a responsible adult.

CONTENTS

What is an Engineer?

An engineer is someone who designs and builds a machine or structure that **solves** a problem. The problem might be that it takes people a long time to get from place to place. An engineer's solution might be a machine like a bicycle or a car …

… or a TRAIN!

Different problems need different kinds of engineer:

- **civil engineers** build roads, bridges, tunnels and public buildings

- **mechanical engineers** build tools, engines and machines

- **electrical engineers** build electrical machines.

To be an engineer, you need to be open-minded, creative and resourceful. You need to be able to picture your ideas in your head, sketch them out on paper, and communicate them to others.

People living on different sides of a river have a problem.

We need a way to meet up!

They can solve this problem by building a bridge.

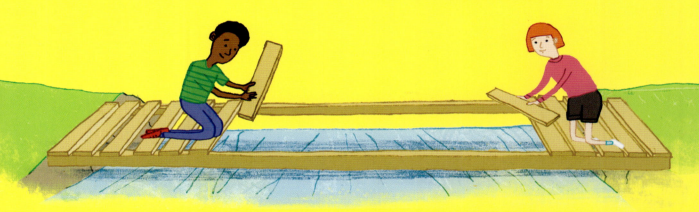

Engineers use a series of steps to achieve their solutions.

1. They ask what the problem is.

2. They imagine a solution.

3. They design, plan and build the project.

4. They review and improve the project.

Do you like the idea of being an engineer? Do you want to be someone who designs and builds solutions to everyday problems?

If so, read this book and begin to train your brain to think like an engineer.

FIND a PROBLEM

Before you can start on an engineering project, you have to decide what the project should be. To do this, you need to identify problems that need solving. And it can't be any sort of problem.

It has to be a problem you can solve by building a structure or machine.

For example, if your problem is that you always wake up late, you could solve it by building an alarm clock.

But if your problem is that you're always feeling tired, it's hard to think of a structure or machine that could help with that.

You should look for a problem with a simple solution – at least
when you're starting out.

For example, there may be engineering solutions to the problem of air pollution,
but they will probably need a lot of time and money. It's best to start by trying
to solve smaller problems.

So how do you find problems that no one has tried to solve yet?

Why not try creating a list of all the things that annoy or bother you.
Ask your friends for their ideas. Here are some suggestions to get you started.

How can you remove
cat hair from clothes?

How do you find the end
of a roll of sticky tape?

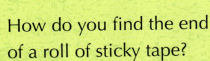

What if there's no
seat available at the
train station?

State the Problem

Once you've found your problem, you need to describe it in a **problem statement**. A problem statement is piece of writing that defines the problem. That means it sets out exactly what the problem is in every detail.

Why is it important to define the problem?

Because if you don't, you might end up building something that doesn't solve the problem.

For example, the problem might be a wobbly table, and your solution might be a wobble-stopper made of cardboard. The trouble is, the table is in the garden. So your cardboard wobble-stopper is fine – until it starts raining!

If you had defined the problem first in all its details, you would have spotted the flaw in your solution.

Your problem statement should answer the following questions:

- Who has the problem? (X)

- What is the problem? (Y)

- Why is it important to solve? (Z)

The problem statement can be written down as follows:
X has a problem with Y because Z.

X has a problem with **Y** because

When writing your problem statement,
ask yourself:

- Do solutions already exist for this problem and do they fully solve it?
How could they be improved?

- Is the problem simple enough for you to create a solution?

- Is it going to be an interesting project to work on?

Charles Kuen Kao: Fibre-optic Pioneer

Sir Charles Kuen Kao was an electrical engineer and a pioneer of fibre-optic communications. This is a way of transmitting information in the form of light beams along thin strands of glass called optical glass fibres. Without Kao's work, we would not have the high-speed phone and Internet access we enjoy today.

Kao was born in Shanghai, China, in 1933. In the 1950s, he moved to the UK where he studied to be an electrical engineer, first at Woolwich Polytechnic (now University of Greenwich) and later at the University of London.

In the 1960s, Kao went to work for Standard Telecommunication Laboratories in Harlow, UK, where he joined the fibre-optics team. Engineers working in this field had hit a problem. When light was sent through optical glass fibres, the light got dimmer the further it went. Many scientists thought this was just what happened to light over long distances. The problem, they said, was caused by an effect called 'scattering'.

But Kao was convinced that the problem could be solved. He predicted that one day glass fibres could be used for long-distance communication. Most experts did not agree. Kao set about trying to prove them wrong.

He believed the problem of the dimming light was caused not by scattering, but by impurities in the glass. He began searching for better materials from which to make the optical glass fibres. Kao visited many glass factories and talked to other engineers and scientists.

In 1969, Kao and his team developed an ultra-transparent form of glass. The light loss for the optical fibres made from this glass was just 4 decibels per kilometre. Previous optical fibres had lost up to 1,000 decibels per kilometre.

Kao had demonstrated that long-distance fibre-optic communications was possible. In 2009, he was awarded the Nobel Prize in Physics for his work, and the following year he received a knighthood. Charles Kao died in Hong Kong, China, in 2018.

Imagine a Solution

Once you've found and defined your problem, you can start to try and imagine a solution. Don't always settle for the first one you think of. If engineers did that, we wouldn't have telephones today, we'd be speaking to each other like this ...

Hello ...

Hello?

Ask yourself: what am I trying to achieve with this solution?
How will I know when I have completed it?
List the **requirements**.
These are the things you want the solution to include.

When you've done that, list the constraints. These are the limitations you face: the amount of money and time you have, the tools, equipment and materials.

Let's say you have a problem with your **school bag** because it's heavy to carry and always hard to find what you need in it.

To solve the problem, you must first decide what you're trying to achieve. List the **requirements**, then the **constraints**.

Requirements:

must be elegant, secure, light and robust.

Constraints:

not much money or time, few tools and materials.

Now list or sketch as many solutions as you can think of. Remember: you don't always need to 'reinvent the wheel'. Look at other solutions to similar problems for inspiration.

Brainstorm

Engineering is often a team effort. People have different skills and unique ways of thinking. When we work with others, we often come up with better solutions than when working alone.

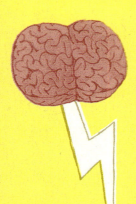

Discussing solutions with others is called **brainstorming.**

When brainstorming, share your ideas with the rest of the group, but also remember to listen to what others have to say. Be **polite** and **respectful** when you give and receive **feedback**. Accept differences of opinion without arguing. **Remember, all ideas are welcome.**

**Think big!
How creative can you be?**

Try brainstorming an idea as a group. Imagine a dam has been built across a river. But there's a problem: migrating fish can no longer pass through the dam to continue their journey upriver.

Divide into three teams. Each team should use the Internet to research one of these solutions:

1. Fish ladder – a series of steps that the fish can leap up

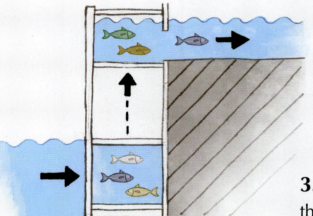

2. Fish elevator – fish swim into a container and are raised over the dam

3. Fish cannon – fish are sent whizzing through a pipe over the dam

Once they've done their research, each team should present their idea and show why it could work. Then brainstorm the best idea.

Brainstorming rules:
- no negative comments   • record all ideas   • build on others' ideas
- stay focused on the topic   • only one conversation at a time.

Don't Be Scared

You may feel shy sometimes when you're in a group. It would be a shame if that stopped you from sharing your ideas. Some of your ideas might be brilliant, but if you don't **communicate** them, they'll never get heard.

I'm not sure if this'll work but …

One reason why people might not want to share their ideas is because they're scared of being wrong or being mocked. But at the brainstorming stage, no one knows what the best solution is yet, so there's no such thing as being right or wrong.

We can't be creative without being brave and putting all our ideas out there to be tested.

All ideas should be welcome.

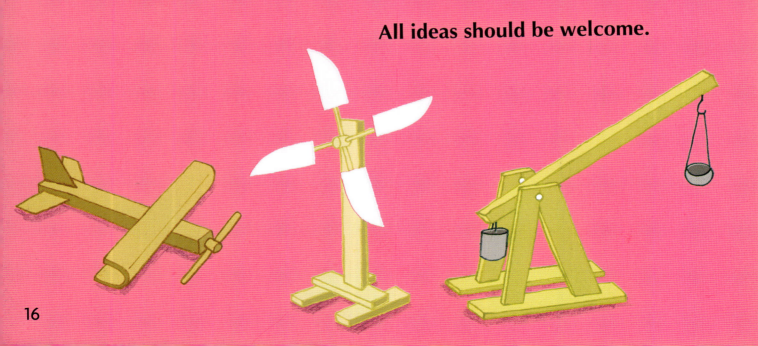

Even if the solution you come up with isn't **practical**, that shouldn't stop you from sharing it. Someone else might have an idea for how to improve it. By discussing it with others, a practical solution might emerge.

Sometimes the hardest thing about putting forward an idea is **choosing the right words**. It may be that you have the idea in your head but you aren't sure how to express it.

To give yourself more confidence, why not trying **writing it down** first so it's clear in your mind before you start talking about it.

Or you could sketch it out!

Break It Down

If you're struggling to find a solution to your problem, it may help to **break it down** into a set of smaller problems. By finding solutions to these smaller problems, you can solve the big problem. Take a bike, for example ...

The bicycle was a solution to an old problem: people wanted a way of moving around more quickly. To solve it, engineers had to solve several smaller problems.

how to steer

how to stop

how to ride comfortably

how to ride uphill and downhill

Engineers break a problem down into its separate parts and look at how they combine to help solve it. This is called systems thinking.

Take any board game and break it down into its different parts.

Dice – tells people how far they can move around the board

Cards – can give players things to do in the game

Board – provides the world in which the game takes place

Player pieces – represent the players on the board

See how the different parts of the game work with each other to solve the larger problem – keeping people entertained!

Here are some other solutions to problems. See if you can break them down into their different parts:

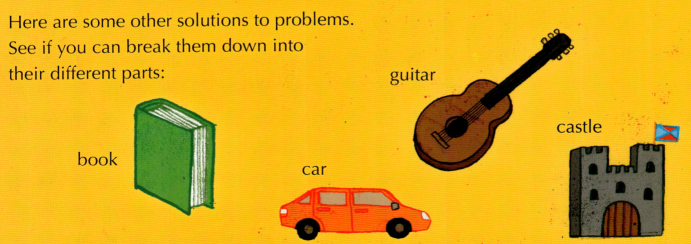

book

car

guitar

castle

Margaret Knight: Prolific Inventor

Margaret Eloise Knight was an American inventor and engineer. She was born in 1838 in York, Maine, and grew up in Manchester, New Hampshire, where she spent her spare time making home-made kites and sleds. After receiving a basic education, she was sent at a young age to work at a cotton mill.

When she was 12, Margaret witnessed an accident at the mill: a worker was injured by a metal-tipped **shuttle** that shot out of the loom. A born engineer, Margaret had seen a problem and couldn't rest until she'd solved it. Within weeks she had developed a safety device to prevent such accidents in future.

In 1867, Knight moved to Springfield, Illinois, where she got a job at the Columbia Paper Bag Company. The following year, she invented a machine that folded and glued paper to form a flat-bottomed paper bag. This was useful as it allowed people to load and unload the bag without holding it. Until then, such bags had to be made by hand.

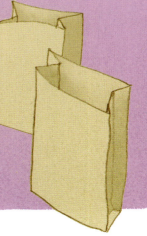

A man called Charles Annan copied Knight's idea and tried to claim it as his own. Knight fought his claim in court and won. She was awarded the **patent** for her invention in 1871. She then established her own paper bag-making company.

Knight continued to invent new devices, including a pair of pliers that could remove lids, a numbering machine, a machine for cutting and sewing shoes, a sliding window, a shield for dresses and skirts, a clasp for robes, and a barbecue spit. In all, she received 27 patents, making her one of the most **prolific** female inventors in US history.

Margaret Knight died in 1914, aged 76. In 2006, she was admitted into the National Inventors Hall of Fame. Her original model of a bag-making machine is still on display in the Smithsonian Museum, Washington, D.C.

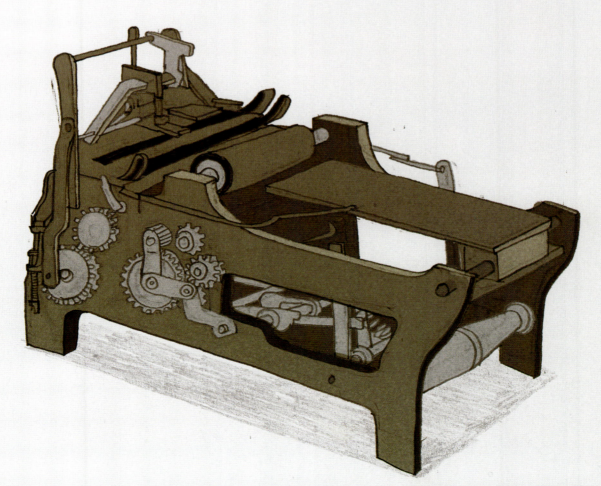

Choose the Best Solution

Once you have your list of possible solutions, you need to work out which one is the best. The 'best' solution may not be the most beautiful or elegant one – it'll be the solution that meets most of your **requirements**, and all of your **constraints**.

Who cares what it looks like? It flies!

It needs to meet all your constraints because these are things (like materials, for example) that you either have or don't have.

Not all your requirements will have equal value. Some will be essential, while others will be nice things to have if possible.

The tower's not essential.

But it's nice to have.

The problem
You want to win a boat-making competition.

Requirements
Boats will be judged on their **strength**, **buoyancy** and **beauty**.

Constraints
You have paper, cardboard, aluminium foil and wood.
You have **one hour** to build it.

Come up with three ideas for boats. Then copy the **decision matrix** below.

Give each **requirement** and **constraint** a score between 0 and 5.
Add them up and find out which solution is the 'best'.

Was it the one you expected?

Requirements and Constraints			
Strength	4	5	
Buoyancy	3		
Beauty			
Building time			

Draw Your Project

Before you build your project, you should create a **drawing** of it. Drawing is a way of sharing the idea in your head with others. If you only describe it using words, you can never be sure other people are imagining what you're imagining.

So, to think like an engineer, start drawing. Keep it simple at first – notice how most objects are made up of **basic shapes**, such as circles and squares. If you can draw these shapes, you can draw anything.

You may have already tried sketching or doodling your project during the brainstorming phase – to show people a very simple version of your idea. Once you've settled on your project, you need to create a more polished drawing of it.

Create your drawing on a large sheet of paper. Include as much detail as you can, so others can see the different parts it's made up of. Your drawing needs to be **accurate** and **in proportion**.
It should include **measurements** and information about what **materials** you plan to use.

You could even create some **storyboards:** sketches showing the device in operation.

All engineering projects are made up of **basic shapes**, such as rectangles, triangles and curved shapes: go out with your sketchbook and look for the basic shapes in the objects you see and try to draw them.

Nikola Tesla: Electric Power Trailblazer

The Serbian-American engineer and inventor Nikola Tesla was born in Croatia in 1856, one of five children. An early inspiration for him was his mother, who invented small household appliances in her spare time. His father wanted him to become a priest, but Nikola was determined to be an engineer. He studied engineering and physics, but did not receive a degree. In 1884, Nikola moved to the USA, where he worked for the celebrated inventor Thomas Edison. The two men soon fell out and parted ways.

These were the early days of electric power, and a problem facing engineers was how to supply electricity over long distances. Tesla developed an electricity supply system called 'alternating current' (AC). His idea received the backing of a businessman, George Westinghouse, who used the AC system to build an electricity supply network.

This put Tesla in competition with his old boss Edison, who championed the rival 'direct current' (DC) system. In the end, Tesla and Westinghouse won the 'battle of the currents'. We use the AC system to this day.

During his career, Tesla experimented with X-rays, wireless power and radio communication. He invented new lighting systems and a radio-controlled boat. Tesla was able to picture an engineering idea in his head with great precision – a technique called 'picture thinking'. He usually didn't make drawings, but worked from memory. This is not possible for most engineers!

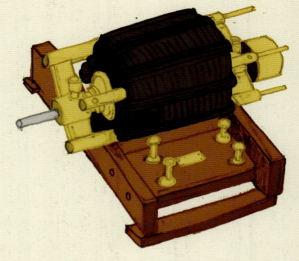

Tesla's induction motor

Radio-controlled boat

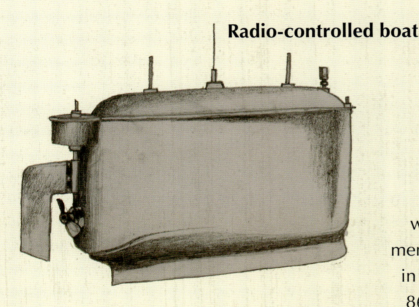

As time went by, Tesla's ideas became more eccentric and impractical. The end of his life was not happy. He suffered from mental illness, and lived alone and in poverty. He died in 1943, aged 86. His legacy lives on, however, in his brilliant engineering ideas. For example, one of his inventions, the Tesla coil, is still used in radio technology today.

The Tesla coil

Plan Your Project

Once you've made a drawing of your project, you may be tempted to move straight to the building stage, but before you get there you should spend a little time **planning** it. This stage is crucial. It's the bridge between the idea on paper and the finished product.

During the planning stage, you need to assemble and test the tools, equipment and materials.

You might realise at this stage that not everything you need is available or affordable, and you need to find replacements. This could mean making some last-minute adjustments to the design.

A paper handbag?

Test the materials you're using. How do they cope under pressure?

Before putting time and effort into building your project,
you could build:
- a **scale model** (smaller version of the project)
- a **prototype** (cheap, rough version of the project)

How about building a **propeller-driven car**? List your requirements.
For example, do you want it to be fast or sturdy? Create a detailed drawing
of the car, then start assembling tools and materials.

For the car project described on pages 30–31, you'll need:

- plastic propellers
- wheels
- straws
- wooden dowels
- craft sticks
- wooden craft blocks
- long rubber bands
- paperclips
- masking tape
- glue

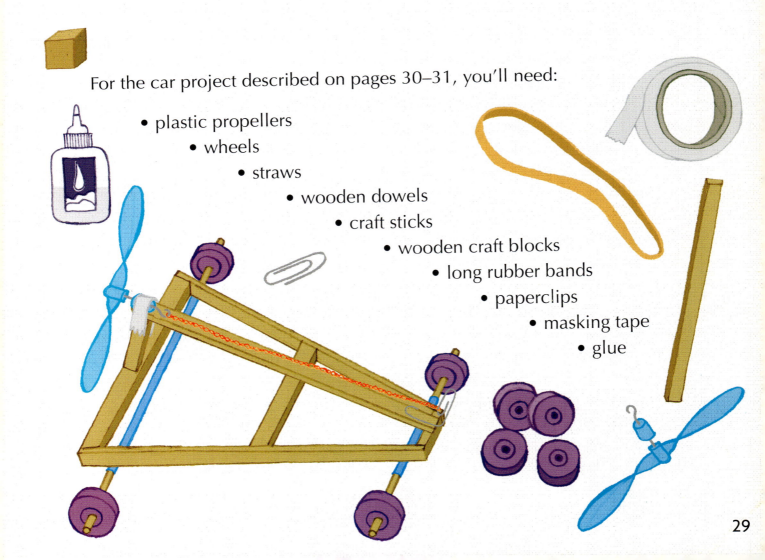

Build Your Project

Now you've drawn and planned your project, it's time to build it! Here are some instructions for building a **propeller-driven car**.

1. Construct the **chassis** with craft sticks.

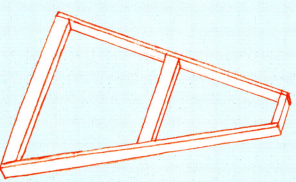

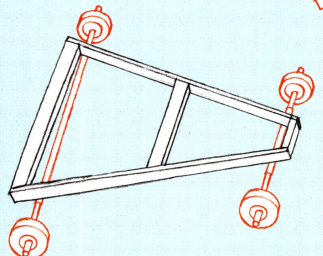

2. Insert wheels on two **dowels** (axles) with a straw in between to keep them apart. Wind tape around the end of each dowel to stop the wheels slipping off. Tape the straws to the chassis, ensuring the dowels inside them can spin freely.

3. Take another craft stick and glue and tape a propeller at one end, and a bent paperclip at the other.

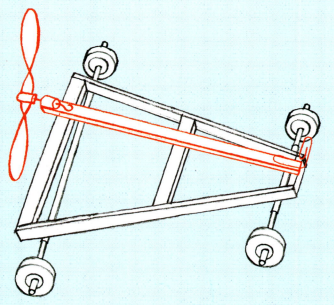

4. Mount the propeller assembly on the chassis at an angle by fixing it to a wooden craft block at one end.

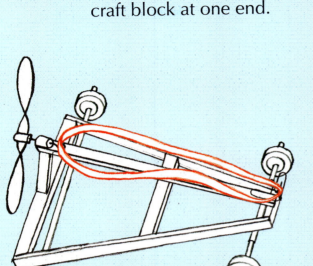

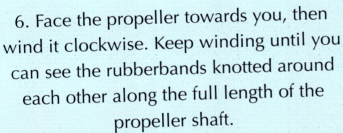

5. Hook two rubberbands between the propeller and the paperclip.

6. Face the propeller towards you, then wind it clockwise. Keep winding until you can see the rubberbands knotted around each other along the full length of the propeller shaft.

7. Hold steady with two hands, then let go!

Don't Be Discouraged

Projects almost never work out perfectly the first time, so don't worry if you fail. It's always a big step moving from the planning to the building stage. When you're drawing the project, you don't have to deal with things like glue on your fingers and broken craft sticks!

You may think you're not cut out to be an engineer. That's called having a closed rather than a growth mindset. Remember, your brain is constantly growing and changing. With practice, your engineering skills will definitely improve.

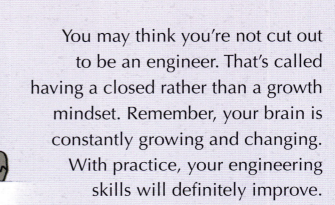

So, ignore the negative voices telling you that you can't do it.

Keep trying and you'll get better. You just need to persevere.

If your project failed,
you might be tempted to start fixing it immediately.
But if you're in a frustrated mood, this might not be the
best time to work on it. You might even make things worse!

Why not take some time out? Put the project aside and go and
do something completely different. You'll know best what sort
of thing helps to calm you down.

You could try **meditating**, **listening to
music** or **reading a book**.

Exercise is always a good option. When your
heart beats faster, it sends more oxygen to
your brain, giving it a boost.

When you come back, you'll
probably be in a much better frame
of mind to deal with the problem.

Review Your Project

Once you've completed a project, you may feel like putting it aside so you can work on something else. Don't be too hasty. Good engineers always **review** their work. It might perform well at first, but how resilient is it?

You can only find out by testing it!

Engineers are not easily satisfied. They want to make sure their projects work again and again without breaking.

Test out your project in different situations and conditions. Does your model car drive smoothly? How does it perform on bumpy, slippery or sloping surfaces?

If you've spotted a problem but can't work out what's causing it, try carefully taking the project apart to work out what the problem is. When you've solved the problem, put it back together again.

It's called reverse-engineering.

Test your propeller-powered car and list any improvements you could make. How well does it meet the original **requirements** for the project?

If it isn't driving smoothly, check the dowels (axles) aren't warped or that glue strands aren't tangled in the axles.

Emily Roebling: Bridge Builder

Emily Warren Roebling was an engineer who helped build one of New York City's most famous landmarks, the Brooklyn Bridge. She was born in Cold Spring, New York, in 1843, the second-youngest of 12 children. In her teens she moved to Washington, D.C. where she received a high-quality education at the Georgetown Visitation Academy.

In 1864, she met a civil engineer named Washington Roebling. The following year they were married. Washington's father, John, was at this time starting work on the Brooklyn Bridge. It would be the longest-span **suspension bridge** in the world at that time.

From the start, Emily took a keen interest in the project. On a trip to Europe following their wedding, Emily and Washington studied caissons – the watertight structures that allowed workers to dig beneath the river to lay the bridge's foundations. In 1869, John Roebling was killed in an accident, and Washington succeeded him as chief engineer on the Brooklyn Bridge project.

In 1872, Washington got very sick and was no longer able to continue working. Emily took over. At first she acted as Washington's spokesperson on the site, passing on his instructions. But as time went by, she displayed such deep understanding of the bridge's construction, people began to accept that she was the chief engineer in all but name. On the day of the bridge's opening in May 1883, Emily was the first to cross it.

Following her work on the Brooklyn Bridge, Emily supervised the construction of a new Roebling family mansion in Trenton, New Jersey. She spent her later years travelling, lecturing and campaigning for women's rights and other causes. She died in 1903, aged 59. Emily Roebling lived at a time when engineering was seen as a man's job, and she had to work extra hard to gain respect. She proved that with the right attitude, anyone can be an engineer.

IMPROVE YOUR PROJECT

Engineers are natural **tinkerers**. To think like an engineer, you should always be looking to **modify** and **improve** projects that you and others have made. Just because it works, it doesn't mean you can't make it work even better!

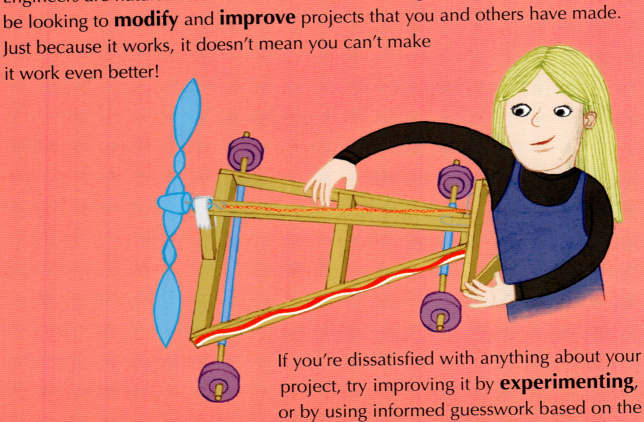

If you're dissatisfied with anything about your project, try improving it by **experimenting**, or by using informed guesswork based on the knowledge you have already gained.

Keep testing and retesting your project every time you make an adjustment. Record your observations in a design notebook.

Try filming it in motion and then slowing down the film to see more clearly what the problems are. Compare it to similar projects made by your friends. What can you learn from each other?

Try making some improvements to your propeller-driven car. Go back to your **requirements**. Did you want it to be **stable** or **fast**?

If you want it to be more **stable**, you could try widening the wheelbase so it's less likely to flip over.

If you want it to be **fast**, try tightening the rubber bands to give it more power.

What happens if you add another rubber band?

Remember: too much power can cause the car to spin out of control!

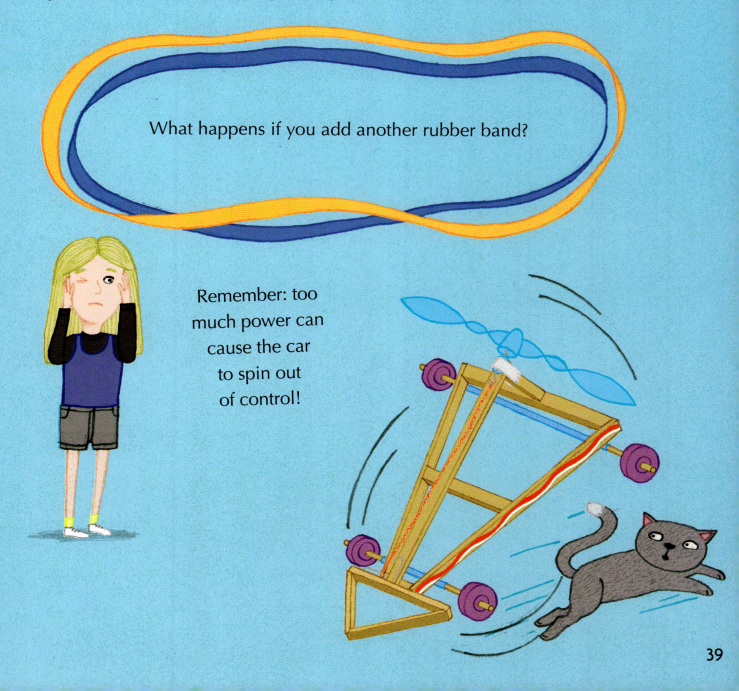

Upcycle

Not every object you build needs to be made out of new materials. Sometimes you can take an object designed for one purpose and **modify** it to make it suitable for another purpose.

It's called upcycling!

This is good news for the planet, as it means we throw away less rubbish.

Upcycling helps to develop your **engineering imagination**. You start looking at everyday objects as raw material for new projects.

Think about this next time you're about to throw out a clothes peg, paperclip, coat hanger, shoebox, lollypop stick, balloon or ping-pong ball.

Could you upcycle it in some way?

Please ask your parent or carer for permission before upcycling anything.

Upcycling an object isn't always simple.
It might involve cutting pieces off, painting or reshaping.

Let's take an ordinary plastic bottle.
How many different uses could you
put it to by modifying it?

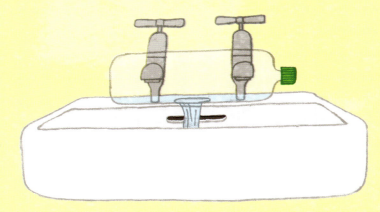

tap mixer

bird feeder

self-watering bottle garden

Can you modify
a plastic bottle
into one of the
following?

• pen holder
• vase
• mobile
• garden sprinkler
• phone holder
• toy rocket

**Before starting, draw the finished project, and assemble the tools
and materials you will need. Then get to work!**

Awesome Engineers

Engineers have shaped our world and pushed the boundaries of what is possible. They've done this by looking at the problems we face and designing solutions for them. Think of some of the everyday problems we face and how they've solved them.

earphones – for listening to music on the go

staples – for joining papers together

umbrella – for rainy weather

phone with GPS – for finding your way

foldable bike – for taking a bike on a train

Engineers are never satisfied with existing solutions and are always striving to improve them. That's why we now have lighter bikes, faster computers, more accurate watches, slimmer phones and wireless earphones.

As you go through your day, think about the objects you use, from a phone charger socket to an airtight container for your sandwiches. Remember: that was once a problem that needed solving. Engineers had to imagine a solution, then design and build it.

A whole history of creativity and imagination lies behind even simple objects like chairs, hats, shoes and lampshades.

We will always need engineers as new challenges arise. They might need to design better masks to shield people from a pandemic, build improved flood defences, or find cheaper ways of harnessing renewable energy because of climate change.

Whatever the problem, engineering will be part of the solution.

You Can Do It!

Are you an imaginative, independent thinker who enjoys solving problems? Are you inspired by the idea of improving people's lives by coming up with creative solutions? In that case, engineering could be for you!

But what problems will I work on? We seem to have machines and devices for just about everything these days!

Yes, but in a changing world, new problems will always emerge. Also, a good engineer is rarely satisfied with existing solutions. There's usually room for improvement.

As you go about your day, list the things that bother you about objects you use. How could they be improved? Keep a notebook of your ideas.

How would you want to shape the world of the future? What sort of world would you like to live in? What kind of machines will it need? What kind of buildings?

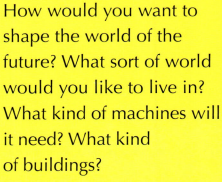

By thinking big and looking at problems in an original way, you can come up with solutions that no one else has thought of. All you need is **imagination**, **persistence** and **dedication**.

Now you've read this book, you've got all the information you need to start thinking like an engineer. So why not try designing and building a project today? The world of engineering is waiting for you.

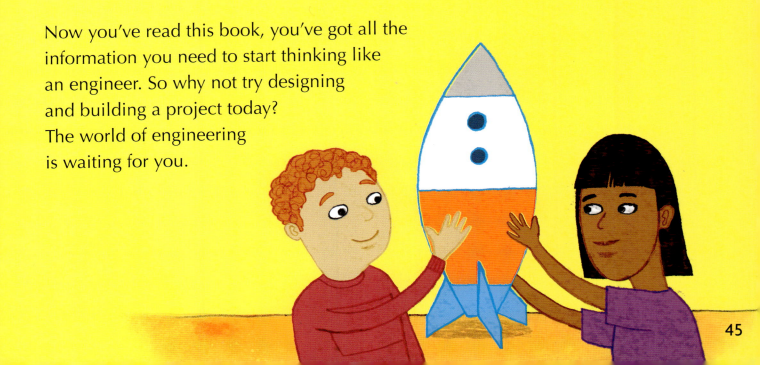

Glossary

assemble gather together in one place

buoyancy the ability of something to float

chassis the base frame of a car or other wheeled vehicle

constraint something that limits you, such as time or availability of materials

decibel a unit used to measure the power of an electrical signal and also the level of sound

decision matrix a chart arranged in rows and columns that you can create to help you decide on the best of a range of options

dowel a thin wooden rod often used when building models

feedback reactions to an idea or suggestion

foundations the lowest part of a building, usually underground, that bears much of its weight

knighthood the title, rank and status of a knight

loom a machine for making fabric by weaving yarn or thread

modify make small or minor changes to something

Nobel prize an international prize awarded each year for outstanding work in various fields

patent an official licence granted to someone, giving them the sole right to make and sell their invention.

practical likely to be successful in the real world

prolific producing many works or ideas

proportion the size of something in comparison to the whole thing; 'in proportion' means that the size of each part of an object is correct compared to other parts and the whole object

requirement something needed or wanted

resilient able to resist and overcome difficult conditions

review check something to see if it can be improved

shuttle a cylinder with two pointed ends for holding yarn, used in weaving

storyboard a sequence of drawings to show the action of something

suspension bridge a bridge in which the weight of the deck is supported by vertical cables suspended from more cables that run between towers

Further Information

Books

STEM-gineers: Experts in Engineering by Rob Colson (Wayland, 2018)
This book looks at the stories, techniques and processes that lay behind the building of some of the world's most spectacular structures.

Awesome Engineering (series) by Sally Spray (Franklin Watts, 2017-19)
This series tells you about some of the most awe-inspiring structures in the world, with illustrations, diagrams and simple text explaining how they were built.

Kid Engineer (series) by Sonya Newland and Izzi Howell (Wayland, 2020-21)
This series introduces readers to the world of engineering with fun, step-by-step projects. There are titles on Machines, Transport, Materials, and Buildings and Structures.

Websites

www.bbc.co.uk/bitesize/subjects/zbb4q6f
This website from the BBC contains lots of informative video clips about engineering. Topics include how to engineer a Formula 1 racing car, digging the world's longest tunnel and designing a safe roller coaster.

www.jamesdysonfoundation.co.uk/resources/design-process-box.html
Scroll down to the bottom of this web page from the James Dyson Foundation to watch some fascinating videos about how to become a design engineer, what makes a good design engineer, and the importance of sketching in the engineering process.

www.youtube.com/watch?v=dOapjyd-4oY
Here are ten fun and simple engineering projects you can do at home, including a balloon-powered car, a rocket and a catapult. The explanations are quick, so get ready to press the pause button!

www.sciencebuddies.org/science-fair-projects/project-ideas/civil-engineering
Here are some ideas for some more complex projects, including a tall tower with a 'shake table', an earthquake-proof bridge and a wall designed for a windy environment.

Index